DOWN

Speeding Star
an imprint of
Enslow Publishers, Inc.

ZOMBIE
ZAPPERS
by Nadia Higgins
Book 4

Library of Congress Cataloging-in-Publication Data

Higgins, Nadia.
  Down, zombie, down! / Nadia Higgins.
    p. cm. — (Zombie Zappers ; bk. 4)
  Summary: "The Zombie Zappers jump back into action when a unique zombie outbreak spreads to their hometown. Leo will have to join forces with Chad's new best friend if they want to stop Rotfield from being overrun by a new breed of zombie"— Provided by publisher.
  ISBN 978-1-62285-015-0
  [1. Zombies—Fiction.] I. Title.
  PZ7.H5349558Dow 2013
  [Fic]—dc23

                          2012028668

Future editions:
Paperback ISBN: 978-1-62285-016-7   EPUB ISBN: 978-1-62285-018-1
Single-User PDF ISBN: 978-1-62285-019-8   Multi-User PDF ISBN: 978-1-62285-146-1

Printed in the United States of America

042013 Lake Book Manufacturing, Inc., Melrose Park, IL

10 9 8 7 6 5 4 3 2 1

To Our Readers:
We have done our best to make sure all Internet addresses in this book were active and appropriate when we went to press. However, the author and the Publisher have no control over, and assume no liability for, the material available on those Internet sites or on other Web sites they may link to. Any comments or suggestions can be sent by e-mail to comments@speedingstar.com or to the address below:

Speeding Star
Box 398, 40 Industrial Road
Berkeley Heights, NJ 07922
USA
www.speedingstar.com

Cover Illustration: Daryll Collins

Table of Contents

1

NEW BEST FRIENDS

Leo Wiley had heard of people who were so happy they woke up with smiles on their faces. He always thought that wasn't a real thing—until it happened to him. On Thursday morning, he woke up with drool dripping down the corner of an actual grin.

Today was the day the Wileys got their new puppy. Leo's stepsister, Shelly, had already named the adorable mutt. "Tina," she'd proclaimed. "She's a perfect Tina."

Visiting the animal shelter a few days before, Leo had looked at the small, tan dog.

And she had looked back at him. A lot of dogs have brown eyes, but these brown eyes were different somehow. They looked smart, as if Tina were about to say something. She had a patch of white fur between her eyes that looked like a Valentine's heart. Her tail had banged a steady beat against the side of the cage.

Getting a dog had been 100 percent Shelly's idea. She was the one who had convinced their parents. She'd made a chores chart for herself. She'd even saved up her babysitting money to pay for dog food and vet bills.

Everybody knew Leo wasn't into "cute" stuff. He was a scientist, a seventh-grade zombie scientist. Still, when Tina was let out of that cage and came straight to him *first*, he hadn't been able help it. He had knelt down and thrown his arms around her neck. She had licked his face until it was shiny wet.

Now, Leo sat up in bed and turned on his phone. He texted his best friend, Chad. *My house after school. Tina's coming!*

In a second, Chad's reply popped up. *Can't, finishing Whiplash at J's house today. It's gonna be awesome!*

And just like that, Leo's grin fell off his face. *J:* That was Jeremy Berry, the most annoying kid at Rotfield Middle School. And no doubt *Whiplash* was one of their dumb robots. That was all Chad seemed to do now, ever since he joined the robotics league last month. Make dumb robots with Jeremy that fell off tables or flung paperclips onto the floor.

Chad *used* to be an awesome zombie artist. He had designed the T-shirts he and Leo sold on their Zombie Zappers Web site. But Chad hadn't come up with a new design since Jeremy became his new best friend.

It's his loss, Leo thought. That's what Leo's mom would say. Chad was the one who was missing out, not him, right?

Still, Leo's grin didn't come back until Tina bounded out of the car after school. She ran right at him. She pushed him over with both paws and licked his face until all his problems went away.

◦ ◦ ◂▬ ◦ ▸

"Cool!"

"No way!"

"Whooooooaaa!"

The next morning, Leo could hear the crowd of kids standing around Jeremy's desk even before he walked into homeroom. Leo looked over. Yup, there was Chad's frizzy brown hair poking up through the middle. Through a gap in the circle, Leo saw Jeremy's arms. Jeremy was operating a remote control on his desk.

Maddie Lee was there too. Leo watched her lean in. She seemed to move in slow motion. That was how she always moved when Leo got the chance to watch her without her knowing it. Leo saw how Maddie's shiny black hair brushed the top of Jeremy's shoulder. "What's it called?" she asked.

"The Whiplash," Chad said in his funniest fake-deep voice.

"Do it again!" Molly Fisher said.

Leo heard a whirring noise. Then he saw a robot moving on tracks like an army tank across Jeremy's desk. Glued on top of the tank was the robotic version of a long spoon.

"It has two XL motors on the flipper for extra projectile capacity." Leo rolled his eyes. That was definitely Jeremy's know-it-all voice.

Jeremy drove the robot to the end of the desk. Just when Leo was sure it was going to drive off the edge, it spun around. A bunch of kids "oooohed" and "ahhhed" as if it were the Fourth of July.

"Here, use this." Maddie giggled a little. She pulled a blue wad of gum out of her mouth and put it in the spoon part of the robot.

"I mounted the flipper on a rotating turret." Jeremy was still going on. Then the spoon thing turned at its base and pointed toward the front of the room.

"Out of the way, people," Chad said, and the circle opened up. "Three . . . two . . . one." Chad pumped his fist in time with his countdown.

"FIRE!" Chad and Jeremy yelled together. The flipper flung back and then forward. *Splat!*

Maddie's gum stuck to the whiteboard at the front of the room.

Maddie was laughing so hard she could barely talk. "Jer-e-mee-ee-eee-eee," she said, hugging her stomach. "That was amazing!"

Then the bell rang, and Ms. Suarez walked in. Maddie ran and scraped her gum off the board. Chad slid into his desk across the aisle from Leo. "Did you see the Whiplash?" Chad whispered. His red face was beaming.

Leo pretended to be looking for something in his backpack. "Not really," he said.

"It was incredible! I'll show you later!" Chad whispered.

But Leo just shrugged and kept digging in his bag.

2

SOMETHING'S WRONG WITH TINA

That Friday afternoon, Leo began another text to Chad about coming to see Tina. But then Leo remembered that day was after-school robotics league. *His loss,* Leo tried to tell himself on the bus ride home. But another thought was louder in his head. *I hate you, Chad Romero,* it said. A*nd you too, Jeremy Berry.*

Leo pulled open the door to his house. "Tina!" he called. He waited a minute. He didn't hear a bark or her nails scraping against the floor. He scanned the yard. There was no sign of her outside either.

"Tiiiinnnnaaaaa!" He yelled louder this time. He walked into the kitchen and hung his backpack on the hook. He checked Tina's bed in the den. Nothing. That was strange. By now she should have been panting dog breath in his face.

"I think Tina's sick." Shelly hurried into the kitchen holding Tina in her arms. The little dog was totally limp. She looked like a bundle of laundry in Shelly's arms.

"Tiiinaaaa," Leo sang softly. He picked up one of her paws and shook it a little. When he let go, it flopped back against Shelly's stomach.

"Mnnnnnnnnnnnnn." Tina made a soft, low moan.

"I'm calling the vet right this instant!" Shelly said. Her voice was squeaky with worry. "Look at her eyes, Leo. She doesn't look at all like herself!" It was true. Tina's brown eyes looked as if they were made of glass.

"It's okay, Tina. Everything's okay," Leo said. He gently petted her ears the way she liked. He looked into the dog's eyes for even a flicker of her old self. But Tina just kept looking right past him.

⚬ ⚬ ⚬ ⚬ ⚬

A few minutes later, Leo was straddling a pile of dirty socks on his closet floor. He knocked softly on the back wall of his closet. "Roger?" he called.

Leo was trying to be more respectful of Roger, one of his best friends. Roger also happened to be a half-zombie. And he happened to live in a secret lab behind Leo's closet. Usually Leo just pressed a button, and the door to the lab slid open with a *swoosh*.

"Ever heard of the word *privacy*?" That's what Roger had said the last time Leo had *swooshed* in without knocking.

Leo had thought of how much he hated when his parents or Shelly barged in on him. "I'm sorry," he had told Roger, and he had meant it.

"Just knock next time, old chap," Roger had replied.

Roger always spoke in a fake British accent. Leo wasn't sure why. But there were a lot of things Leo didn't know about Roger, actually. This was true despite the fact that the boys had been friends for more than four years now.

Leo and Roger had met at a T-ball game the summer after second grade. Roger was already a half-zombie by then, though nobody knew. He'd been only licked—not fully bitten—in the zombie attack that had wiped out his family. With lots of Band-Aids and the right outfit, Roger could pass as a fully living person.

But there were risks. The day of the T-ball game, for example, Roger's ear fell off in a blast of wind. Luckily, Leo was the only one who noticed. Leo picked up the floppy greenish ear with his bare hands. He didn't feel grossed out at all. Even then, Leo was a zombie scientist at heart. That day, Roger came home with Leo, and Leo glued his ear back on. Then the two friends broke ground on the secret lab that became Roger's home.

Swooosh. "M'boy!" Roger's greenish face looked less zombie-like than usual today. In fact, it was bordering on perky. "To what do I owe this pleasure?"

"*You're* in a good mood," Leo said, sighing a little.

"And *you* look downright droopy. No Chad again today, I'm afraid?" Roger said. He patted Leo on the shoulder.

"All he wants to do is make dumb robots with Jeremy. Plus, Tina's sick," Leo said. He flopped down on a box labeled with the words "THIS WAY UP" and an arrow pointing at his knees. "Roger?" Leo rested his head against his hand. "Do you think Chad still wants to be friends with me?"

"I gather yes. But Leo . . ." Roger smiled pleasantly at his friend. "That depends on you as well."

"Me?" Leo said. "I didn't do anything!"

"You know, Leo," Roger said, "robots *can* be rather interesting."

Leo rolled his eyes. "Not as interesting as zombies."

Roger laughed a little. "True, true!" he said. He was positively grinning now.

"Roger, that smile's about to crack your face in half," Leo remarked. How did Roger do it? He had problems with a capital *P*. Yet he almost always seemed so cool.

"I *am* rather bursting with excitement," Roger said. His eyes were bulging. He looked like a really happy (though slightly rotten) frog. "Have you heard the latest reports from the Uranus space probe? They've found Z-rays in the inner atmosphere!" Roger clapped his hands carefully.

"Really?" Leo said, perking up. He and Roger had been looking for evidence of Z-rays for a long time. Most scientists believed the ultrahigh-frequency waves were just a myth. Not Roger. Not only did he believe they existed, but he also thought they held the cure to his own half-zombiehood.

"Does that mean—?" Leo began.

"I've already started!" Roger said. He picked up an object from the floor by his feet. It was a simple silver pole with a silvery ball on top. "Introducing the world's first Z-ray maser!" Roger said. He held out his invention like a trophy.

"Masers can be very tricky machines, indeed." Roger said. "Doesn't look like much, does it? But the plasma inside this ball is spinning at record speeds." Roger shook the thing a little. "Or it will be when I'm done."

"You mean that machine makes invisible Z-waves?" Leo held out his hand to take the device for a closer look.

"Well, no, not quite," Roger said. "I admit I'm having trouble creating the frequency. But I'm close, m'boy. So very close!"

CHAPTER

3

ANYTHING BUT FINE

L uckily, Leo had Roger's good news to keep him happy. Because by the next day, Saturday, Leo's life was only getting worse. The vet had no idea what was wrong with Tina. And she was getting weirder. She tried to bite Dad's calf as he came out of the shower. Then Mom freaked out and put Tina on a leash outside.

"I don't want her inside while we're gone," Mom said. "She's too dangerous." Leo's mom and dad were leaving to go to a talk about mortgages, or maybe it was garages. That meant Tina would be outside the whole day.

"But it's cold!" Shelly shrieked.

"We'll leave the shed open for her," Dad said in his "I'm serious" voice. "She'll be fine."

But Tina looked anything but fine when Leo stepped outside after breakfast. Saturday morning meant it was Leo's turn to feed the chickens at Mr. Smith's coop next door. "Hey Tina," he said softly as he started across the yard. He held out his hand to her, but she just snarled and snapped.

Leo checked his phone as he walked across Mr. Smith's dewy grass. There was one text from Chad: *Almost done with new robot. Can't wait to show you. Gonna be epic!*

Leo thought about what Roger had said. Maybe robots could be cool. *If only Chad's robots didn't come with Jeremy included*, Leo thought. He shoved the phone into his pocket without replying.

That was strange. Leo was almost to the coop, but he didn't hear any clucks or coos from the chickens. Usually the hungry chickens were waiting for him in the fenced-off area around the coop. Leo grabbed the feed from Mr. Smith's shed and opened the wire gate to their outdoor pen. "Goldy! Mandy! Louise! Penny!" Leo called out softly. Had they flown away? Had they been eaten? Stolen? Leo searched for signs of a break-in. He looked back toward his own yard. There was Tina, pulling at her leash, but definitely still tied up. The pen seemed nice and neat. *Too neat.*

Leo walked into the little white coop with the green roof. He stood there for a minute. He waited for his eyes to adjust to the shadows as he scanned the little room. No, the chickens weren't on their nests. They were—

Thwack! Leo felt a brush of feathers against his ankle. *Thwwwoooop!* Now feathers on his face and—ouch! Pecking on his calves and butt and arms. Leo spun around as feathers floated and twirled in the air around him. He kicked and waved his arms. He pulled off the chickens with his hands and flung them across the room. But one hung on. She gripped the edge of his sleeve with her beak.

"Goldy?" Leo spoke softly to the orange chicken dangling over his hand. But the bird just looked past Leo with empty eyes.

"Mnnnnnnnnnnnnn." She made a low, deep moan. Green puss oozed from a gash between her eyes. It streamed down her feathers and her beak. It coated the flap of red skin under her chin and dripped onto Leo's hand.

UNSPEAKABLE THINGS

L eo ran all the way home. "Roger!" He panted as he knocked on the back of his closet wall.

Swoosh! "What is it?" Roger was holding his Z-ray maser in one hand.

Leo tried not to yell as he told Roger what he'd just seen. "Tina and Mr. Smith's chickens . . . they're acting like . . . zombies!" So was the Carlsons' cat that Leo had jumped over on his way home. And Moxie, the poodle across the street, who was drooling green stuff on the Dokas' window. "Can that be, Roger? Can animals be zombies? I mean, it's possible, right?" Leo leaned against a wall to catch his breath.

"Extremely rare," Roger said. He sat down on his favorite box and didn't say anything for a minute. When he spoke, he looked as if he were examining something very far away. "In fact, I know of only one certified case. In that instance, the outbreak began with animals. At first, everyone thought it was an animal-only infection. Not typical, but not unheard of. Then, after several days, it spread to humans. A case of cross-species zombification. Extremely rare." Roger absently rubbed the silver ball between his hands. "But no less devastating."

Was that a tear sliding down Roger's greenish face? Leo's own face suddenly felt hot. He coughed a little and stared at his feet. "Um, are you okay?" Leo asked.

"You see," Roger continued. He stared into the distance. "The incident of which I speak was, as you may have guessed, my own. The zombie outbreak that wiped out my town, my family, and yes, my pet turtle, Amelia."

There was so much Leo had always wanted to ask Roger about his past. But Roger didn't like to talk about it. He referred to it as his "unspeakable time." It was now or never, Leo thought. He took a deep breath and looked up. "What caused it, Roger? I mean, what caused the zombies in your town?"

"No one is certain," Roger said. "But I believe there was an alien influence." He spoke softly but in his usual way, as if he didn't mind too much that Leo had asked.

"Like, outer space aliens?" Leo said.

"Indeed," Roger said. "My current belief is that an irregular wave pattern from Uranus was the trigger."

"Um, Roger," Leo continued. There was another question Leo had always been too afraid to ask. "How did it end? I mean how did your family, um, stop existing, exactly?"

"The authorities put them out of their misery," Roger said.

"You mean police came and killed the zombies?" Leo asked. Was there a better way he was supposed to say that?

"In a manner of speaking," Roger said.

"How?" Leo couldn't stop now. "Did they shoot their brains like in the movies?" Leo cringed. There definitely had to be a better way to say *that*.

But Roger was smiling. He shook his head. "No, no, my dear fellow. That's just fiction. You can't kill zombies by destroying their brains. A totally unproven method."

"Really?" Leo asked. "Yes, and thank goodness. Scientists at the Braindale Institutes of Science came up with a much, shall we say, *cleaner* plan. Not a plan to cure the zombies, of course. There was no time for that. But they found a way to stop the outbreak." Roger closed his eyes for a long time, and Leo didn't dare ask the question that was exploding inside his brain.

At last, Roger opened his eyes and spoke again. "They blasted the zombies with Y-rays. And the zombies, as you say, stopped existing."

"Were you there, Roger? Did you see it?"

"No," Roger said. "I had fled by then. Likely a good thing, don't you think?"

"Leo? Leo, where are you? Leeeeeeeooooooo! . . . Leo, I've been calling you!" Shelly was standing in the doorway of the lab. "Whoa, why the long faces?" Then, without waiting for an answer, Shelly squeezed next to Roger on his box. "Hi, Rogie, whatcha working on?" Shelly had had a not-so-secret crush on Roger ever since he'd cured her of temporary zombiehood last year.

"Leo? Leeeeooooo!" Now Chad's voice was calling from downstairs.

"Oh, that's right," Shelly said, turning ever so slightly from Roger. "Chad and Jeremy are here. They have some kind of robot to show you."

Leo sighed. He glanced at Roger, who looked a bit greenish-pink but not unhappy. "Coming!" Leo called.

"Check it out!" Chad and Jeremy were sitting around the kitchen table. This time, Chad was holding the remote control. Jeremy watched intently with his squinty face.

"Hi Chad. Hi . . . Jeremy." Leo stood a few feet away. "What's this?" On the table was a green humanoid robot that seemed to be wearing tan pants and a plain T-shirt. It had a red stripe painted across its neck. A hole in the middle of the T-shirt had been stuffed with green jelly, or maybe mashed grapes? The robot was taking slow, jerky steps toward Shelly's empty cereal bowl.

"Can't you tell?" Jeremy said.

"Uh . . ." Leo looked at the robot for another second. "Is that supposed to be a scarf?" He pointed at the red stripe on the robot's neck.

"No!" Chad was obviously offended. "C'mon, dude. Look again."

"Um. . . what's that green stuff?" Leo asked.

"Slime!" Chad said, giggling a little. "We're still working on increasing the sliminess."

Click, click, click. The robot made slow steps across the table as Leo tried to figure out what to say next. "Um, does it go faster?" he finally asked.

"It's not *supposed* to go faster!" Jeremy swiped up the robot with a huff.

"It's a Zombot, Leo. Get it? A zombie robot!" Chad said. "See? There's blood, slime. I thought it'd be great merchandise for the Web site."

"Um . . ." Leo didn't seem to be able to say anything else. He put his hands in his pockets and twisted one sneaker into the floor.

"Forget it, Leo," Chad said. "Just forget it. C'mon, Jeremy."

Jeremy and Chad grabbed their jackets off the back of a chair and left the house without another word. As the door clicked shut, Leo closed his eyes. Wrong, wrong, wrong! There *had* to be a better way to have handled that, he thought.

Slam! Leo opened his eyes. Chad and Jeremy were back inside the kitchen. They leaned against the closed door. Their eyes were wide. Their chests moved up and down with panting breaths. Chad's face was red and shiny with sweat. Jeremy looked liked an overcooked noodle. He slumped down, and the Zombot in his hand clattered to the floor.

"Zombies . . . attacking . . . NOW!" Chad gasped. He pointed with his chin out the window as his hands fumbled with the bolt on the kitchen door.

5

ZOMBIE ATTACK

L eo heard them before he saw them. A chorus of moaning, clucking, growling, squeaking, snorting, gurgling, clicking, and deranged purring. All the sounds were familiar but wrong somehow. The sounds crawled up and down Leo's skin. They crept inside his ears like living things.

Leo ran to the kitchen window. If this had been a movie, he would have poked Chad in the ribs. The boys would have snorted at what they saw. But here, in real life, the sight felt like an avalanche. A slow-motion avalanche of dread coming straight for him.

Leo's legs started shaking as he took in the scene. The street was completely filled with pets. It was dogs mostly, but lots of cats too. He saw gerbils, hamsters, ferrets, fish, lizards, snakes, spiders, crabs, and some kind of caterpillar that looked like bird poop with legs. The pet zombies walked, slithered, crept, wobbled, and dragged their limp bodies in slow, jerky motions. They moved like an animal zombie band marching in time to some sick pet whistle that only they could hear.

As the parade got closer, Leo gagged. The smell of rotting animal flesh mingled with the smells of all the other stuff seeping from their bodies. Gashes slashed across their fur, feathers, and scales. Some gashes dripped red blood. Others oozed green puss or syrupy black liquid. Gobs of silky pink guts and wrinkled brains were scattered on the street like zombie litter.

Closer and closer they came. Frozen in place, Leo made out more details. A poodle with a gerbil gnawing on its butt. A cat with another cat's leg sideways in its mouth. A parrot with its head dangling by one blue vein.

Oh no. Leo felt his breakfast bubbling up his throat. Then—*Smack! Smack! Smack!* Something was at the window. It was beating against the glass just inches from his face. A lightning-shaped crack spread across the pane. *Smack!* It was a dog's paws. *Smack!* Two bloody paws with a face between them. *Smack!* Glassy brown eyes separated by a white fur heart.

"Tina!" Shelly was there now, screaming behind Leo.

Then Tina's paw came crashing through the glass. Leo pulled his face back as Tina slashed at the air in front of him. Then Roger's arm crossed in front of Leo's eyes. Roger pushed Tina's paw back through the glass.

A flash of silver, and Chad had sealed the hole with duct tape.

"That will do for now," Chad said. He stood with his legs apart, arms folded across his chest. He looked around the kitchen. "Okay, listen up, everybody!" He pulled Jeremy to his feet, and Leo, Roger, and Shelly made a circle around him. Chad had clearly gone into full zombie-fighter mode. That made Leo feel a little braver himself.

"It appears the zombie pets are coming straight for Leo's house," Chad said. "We're not sure why or how to stop them. We'll deal with that later. First step: defense. Leo, board up windows. Get wood, nails, hammers. More duct tape! Jeremy, we'll move the furniture against the doors." Chad walked into the living room and started pulling on one end of the Wileys' plaid sofa.

"Shelly, you're in charge of armor: gloves, hats, long sleeves. Leather is best. Anything to protect from bites. Roger, you start on weapons," Chad continued. "Baseball bats, obviously. But be creative. Think brooms, lamps, chairs, spatulas, spray bottles! Anything that will buy us time. PUSH!" Chad barked at Jeremy, who was leaning weakly against the other end of the sofa.

Then Leo didn't have time to be scared anymore. Even though a German shepherd ate a hole through the TV room wall. And a zombie cat tore off the storm door with its jaws. And a zombie snake squeezed halfway under the back door. It took Roger several minutes to push the snake back out with a cookie tray.

Leo worked until all the nails and wood scraps in the basement were gone. Then he found his mother's hot glue gun in the bottom of the craft drawer. He used that to put up whatever wood pieces he could find: firewood, 3-D puzzle pieces, the slats holding up his mattress. He even used up last few wood blocks he'd kept from when he was a little kid.

Little by little, the animal zombie sounds grew quieter. The *thwacks* turned into thuds, and the crashing turned to scratching. As Leo covered the windows, the house grew darker. The zombie animal parade was blocked from view. But the wood boards Leo put over the windows weren't going to last long, he could tell. They looked like living things as they bent in and out. They began to splinter as the zombie animals pushed from the other side.

6

AN EXCELLENT IDEA

The Zombie Zappers gathered in the living room. "What next?" Jeremy whispered. He had helped Chad push all the furniture against the walls and doors. Still, he looked completely white. He sat on the floor and pulled his knees to his chest.

"We have to stay cool," Chad said.

"We must think," Roger added.

Shelly said, "We need a plan."

The group sat in silence for a few minutes. *Bang!* One of the boards flew off the window and crashed onto the floor. A giant dog's shaggy head shot through the gap in the window. *Nnnnnrrrr,* it growled. Its eyes looked like spinning red marbles. Blood dripped down its white fur in wavy streaks.

NNNNNNnnnnnrrr. The zombie dog tried to push its body farther inside. Instead, its head got stuck between the boards. *NNNNNNRRRR!* The dog tore at the boards with its teeth. In a rage, it spat bloody chunks of wood into the room. One of them smacked Jeremy on the cheek. Roger fought the dog back with a rolling pin while Leo and Chad nailed the board back into place.

"It won't hold," Chad said as he frantically layered duct tape over the board's edges.

Jeremy whimpered. With one hand, he clawed at the bloody spot on his cheek where the wood had smacked him. With the other, he hugged the Zombot as if it were a teddy bear.

For the first time ever, Leo felt sorry for Jeremy Berry. Jeremy looked about five years old in his oversize hoodie and bright white sneakers. He cried softly to himself, rocking on his butt.

Somehow, with Jeremy that scared, Leo couldn't be scared at all. There couldn't be two of them in la-la freak-out land. No, Leo's brain seemed to be in perfect working order. *Think*, he told himself, and he could. What had caused the zombie outbreak? That was the first question. With a cause came a solution. What were the facts?

Leo thought about the past few days. He remembered when Tina first started acting strange. That was yesterday—Friday. The same day as Roger's goofy grin and his Z-ray maser. Then Leo remembered what Roger had said about the zombie outbreak in his town four years ago. How it had started with animal zombies. How Roger believed it had to do with irregular waves.

"I know what caused this!" Leo said, jumping to his feet. "Roger!" he yelled. "It's the Z-ray maser! It's turning pets into zombies and luring them here. Turn it off! Turn it off!"

But Roger sat just as still as before, cross-legged on the Wileys' orange carpet. "I believe you are right," Roger said. "It makes sense. However, I'm afraid the damage has been done. Even if I turn it off, it's too late. Perhaps I could change the frequency and reverse the damage . . ." Roger shook his head sadly. "But I need time, days at least."

"Hold up!" Chad was walking in a circle around the others. He held an arm out in front of his head as if to catch the idea that was obviously growing inside his brain. "I know!" Chad punched the air. "I know! Leo!" Chad turned to face his friend. "You say

Roger's laser—or whatever it is—is luring the zombies here?"

"Yes," Leo said slowly. He was already starting to catch on to what Chad was thinking. Just like old times.

"So that means if we can move it, it could lure the zombies away from here . . . to somewhere else?" Chad continued.

"Yes," Leo said again, but he didn't sound certain. He looked around the room with the furniture against the doors and all the windows boarded up. He watched the wood splintering as the zombies tried to get inside. "But how?" How would they get the Z-ray maser out of the house and past the zombies? "It's too dangerous," Leo said.

"Un-uh." Jeremy had stopped rocking and was shaking his head a little. "No, it's not dangerous." Jeremy leaned forward. He unhugged the Zombot and held it out with one hand. "I know how to do it."

Jeremy stood up and started pulling electronic parts out of his pockets. "Of course, I'll need a laptop and a Wi-Fi connection. I'll need batteries, wire—preferably eight-gauge, maybe a fuse. Do you have one? Oh, and a spare switch." Jeremy pulled out a square part with shiny green computer chips halfway up one side. "This GPS receiver module should work just fine. Now all I need is something for the wings. Something light and strong."

"Wings?" Leo asked.

"For flying the Zombot!" Chad practically jumped up and down with every word. "We can attach Roger's Z-ray thingy and fly it over the zombies' heads! Right, Jeremy?"

"Right," Jeremy said. He continued muttering to himself, "and glue and electrical tape, maybe." Jeremy organized the contents of his pockets on a dining room chair.

"What an excellent idea!" Shelly pronounced.

Leo had to agree. In fact, it wasn't even hard to agree, not now, not with every zombie pet in Rotfield eating his house. "That sounds awesome," Leo said. He went to the closet and pulled out the bright yellow Windbreaker his mom made him wear when he rode his bike on busy streets. "Would this work for wings?" He shoved the wadded-up jacket under Jeremy's nose.

"Definitely," Jeremy said, adding it to his pile of equipment.

For a moment, nobody said anything. Relief spread over the zombie fighters' slightly smiling faces. Every pet zombie in Rotfield still wanted to tear off their skin and feast on their guts. But they had a plan.

7

DO NOT PANIC

"**S**cissors! Can I get some scissors over here?" Jeremy yelled, snapping his fingers over his head. But nobody moved as relief was overtaken by another, more familiar feeling: worry. Slight worry that bubbled into real worry and then burst into panic because a new sound joined the chorus of animal zombie noises outside.

All the zombie fighters grabbed their stomachs as a whooshing, beating noise rattled the house. What *was* it? It was familiar somehow, though they'd never heard it in real life before. It was a sound from the movies. It grew louder and louder and louder until it was just a roar. The roar of a helicopter hovering above the house.

"Attention! Attention!" a voice boomed over a megaphone. "This is the police. Don't panic! I repeat, do not panic."

Later, Leo would remember this moment as if it really were a scene from a movie. Because everything went slow motion and quiet in his head. And he had the most random thought. *Is that irony?* He remembered the word from English class. *The use of words to express the opposite of what they intend.* Because the more the police shouted, "Do not panic!" the more he felt like screaming.

"Assault to begin in T minus one minute!" the voice boomed. "Proceed to the basement IMMEDIATELY. Repeat: Assault to begin. Remove yourself from the line of fire. And DO NOT PANIC!"

Leo ran to the window. "No! Don't shoot!" he screamed. "Don't shoot. It won't work! Don't shoot!" But there was no way the police could hear him. Not over the sound of the helicopter and through the boarded window. Leo started tearing at the wooden slats with his bare hands until his arms were scratched and bloody.

"We have a plan! Please, please, don't shoot! Don't shoot! Don't shoot Tina!" He was crying now. His whole body shuddered with each gulping sob. He managed to push one bleeding arm through a crack in the boards. Then he felt something behind him wrap around his waist and pull. He fell on his back, waving his arms and legs like an upturned bug.

"Settle down, Leo," came Chad's voice from underneath him. Chad had both arms underneath Leo's armpits. "C'mon. Settle down." Chad didn't sound mad, just loud, as if he was trying to cover up how scared he really was.

Leo let out a long, shuddering breath, and Chad let go. Leo sat up to see Roger snapping a pair of salad tongs. A gerbil with brains coming out of one ear was squeezing through the crack Leo had made. Roger pushed it back with the salad tongs and repaired the crack.

"Sorry," Leo said weakly.

"It's quite all right," Roger said. Roger rubbed his own face the way Leo's dad did when he had a headache. "May I have your attention, everyone?" Roger said to the group. He leaned for a second against the back of a dining room chair. "I'm afraid I know what is to be done." Then, looking at Shelly, he sighed and continued, "I hope you will all understand."

"No!" Shelly yelled. "You can't do it!"

"Do what?" Chad asked.

"I don't know!" Shelly said. "But I don't like it! Not one bit!"

"Please, try to understand," Roger repeated as he walked toward the staircase. He stood on the first step and turned around. "My dear friends," he said, "I'm off to the roof. My hope is that the authorities will see me and pull me up. Then I can explain our predicament. It is our only hope."

Then, as if on cue, the voice from the helicopter boomed: "T minus thirty seconds. Evacuate to the basement. I repeat, evacuate. And do not panic!"

Roger turned to Jeremy and Chad. "Please, continue working on the Zombot. There is no time to lose."

"No, please, Rogie!" Shelly's voice squeaked on *Rogie.* "It's too dangerous!"

"For any of you, perhaps," Roger said, smiling a bit. "But not for me."

Of course, Roger was right. Leo knew exactly what he meant. If Roger got shot or fell off a roof, he'd be okay with a Band-Aid or two, or some Krazy Glue. But the rest of them would be goners.

Sure, Roger could get bitten by a zombie bird, and who knows what that would do. And Roger's secret half-zombie identity might very well be revealed. But still . . .

"He's right," Leo said. "He's our best hope." Leo walked toward Roger, who was slowly making his way up the stairs. Leo grabbed a crowbar from the pile of weapons at the bottom of the stairs. "I'll get the window for you, my dear brave friend," he said, doing his best imitation of Roger's fake British accent. He bounded up ahead of his half-zombie friend, two steps at a time.

"Much appreciated," Roger called up after him, taking another careful step.

8

ZOMBOTS AND Z-RAYS

Shelly caught up with Leo in the attic. Leo remembered just how tough his stepsister could be during life-or-death zombie attacks. She knew Roger was right, and she'd admit it later. Right now, she didn't say anything. She squeezed her lips together as she helped Leo pry the wooden planks off the attic window.

By the time Roger joined them, everything was ready. Roger hadn't grown since second grade, so he easily fit through the small opening. He scaled up to the pointy rooftop and perched on the edge. His feet rested on the slopes that slanted down from either side. Roger waved his arms over his head. "Yooo-hoooo," he called. "Helllooooo."

Apparently the police weren't used to seeing slightly green-skinned kids waving to them from rooftops. Before any zombie birds could get close, a rope lowered from the helicopter. Roger began to slowly inch his way up.

"Check it out!"

Leo turned and saw Chad's arm poking up through the attic hatch behind him. Chad was holding the Zombot, which now had bright yellow wings. Its arms were out straight in front of it. The Zombot carried the Z-ray maser as if the robot were a tray with dinner on it.

A second later, Chad and Jeremy joined Leo and Shelly at the open attic window. "It's all tested, 100 percent operational," Jeremy said. He wasn't smiling, but he seemed excited in his own serious way. Jeremy pulled out the remote control that was sticking sideways out of his hoodie pocket. "Initiate launch!"

Shelly peered out the open window. "Coast is clear!" she reported.

"Three . . . two . . ." Chad pumped his fist in time with his countdown. Jeremy pressed a button, and the Zombot's motor started to whir. "One . . . BLASTOFF!"

Chad thrust the Zombot out the window on his open palm. For a moment, it hovered in the air above his hand. It spun in crazy circles as Jeremy frantically pressed buttons on the remote. Then it went still all at once. And it began to fly. Its bright yellow wings became a blur as the Zombot drifted gracefully over the Wileys' roof.

"Jolly good, mates!" Roger's voice called out from the top of the helicopter's rope. Then Roger was being pulled inside the helicopter. Through the helicopter window, Leo saw the back of Roger's head. His hands were moving in circles the way they always did when he was making an important point. Leo saw the two blue police hats nodding up and down as Roger talked.

"It's working! It's working!" Chad screamed. The zombie animals unstuck their claws and teeth from the side of the Wileys' house. They turned their heads to the sky, as if picking up a scent. The zombies turned and started lurching down the Wileys' driveway. The helicopter's roar began to lessen as the police followed the animal zombies down the street.

"Where are you taking the zombies?" Leo asked Chad. They hadn't had time to work out that part of the plan.

"Oh, I have the perfect place," Chad said, grinning, and even Jeremy smiled. "C'mon, we'll show you."

Chad led the way back down the attic hatch and to the kitchen door. Shelly pulled the china cabinet away from the door. The Zombie Zappers slid sideways out the door and into a beautiful fall day.

Leo looked up. The Zombot was becoming a yellow dot in the blue sky. Below it, the animal zombies jerked and dragged their bodies down to the end of the block. But Leo knew everything was going to be okay. Roger would keep the police from shooting the zombies. Jeremy's robot would keep flying long enough for Chad to guide the zombies to a safe spot. Then Roger would have time to fix the

Z-ray maser. Shelly would make sure of that. And Leo?

Leo listened to the chorus of moaning, clucking, growling, squeaking, snorting, gurgling, clicking, and deranged purring. He watched a chicken slip on a pile of intestines as if it were a banana peel. He saw a fish swimming in a stream of blood. He saw a cat eat—and then barf up—Moxie the poodle's shiny pink jacket.

"Aaaaaahhhaaaa-haaaaaa-hhhhaaaaa-ha-ha!" Leo's laughs burst out him like water breaking through a dam. "Ha-haaa-haaaaaaaa!" It felt so good. He tilted back his head and let his laughs rip.

That made Chad snort, which made Jeremy's shoulders shake, which made Shelly wheeze and hug her stomach.

"C'mon, run!" Chad said. Still laughing, Leo, Shelly, and their friends chased after the flying zombie robot and the parade of Rotfield's pet zombies streaming beneath it.

EPILOGUE

C had *did* have the best idea. He led the zombies to Rotfield Middle School. Since it was Saturday, the building was completely empty. Jeremy flew the Zombot into the gym, and the zombies followed. Then the police secured the doors. For now, the zombies—and Rotfield—were safe.

By the end of Saturday, everybody in Rotfield knew about Roger's no-longer-secret half-zombiehood. But given the circumstances, nobody freaked out on him. Not even Leo's parents, exactly.

"You could have trusted us," Leo's dad said when he found out about Roger's whole story and the secret lab.

"You *can* trust us," Leo's mom said. "We are so very proud of you," she added, giving Roger a squeeze around the shoulders.

School was cancelled that Monday *and* Tuesday. That gave Leo, Chad, and Jeremy time to perfect the flying Zombot. It would become an all-time best seller on the Zombie Zappers Web site. The three friends had so much fun that Leo forgot why he hadn't liked Jeremy in the first place.

On Wednesday, Roger finally fixed the Z-ray maser. He created just the right Z-wave frequency to cure the zombie pets. That afternoon, Tina came back home. She jumped onto Leo and licked his face until it was shiny wet.

Roger believed "with great certitude" that the Z-ray maser would cure him as well. But somehow, he felt nervous about pressing that magical button on his invention. "I've been this way for so long," Roger said. "I can barely remember what it feels like to be human."

Then, that very night at dinner with the Wileys, Roger got an important call. It was the head of the Braindale Institutes of Science. Would Roger report to duty right away? A zombie outbreak had been reported on the north side of town.

Leo's dad was happy to drive Roger to his assignment. Grinning, Roger simply stood up and walked out the door to the car. "I don't even have to pack a bag," he remarked.

It was true. As a half-zombie who barely slept or ate or went to the bathroom, Roger didn't need pajamas or a toothbrush or clean underwear. For now, Roger would stay just the way he was, half-zombie superpowers intact.

Read each title in ZOMBIE ZAPPERS

ZOMBIE CAMP
ZOMBIE ZAPPERS BOOK 1

Get to know Zombie Zappers Leo, Chad, and the rest of the gang as they try to solve the mystery of the Smellerd zombies at summer camp. What nightmarish surprise will they find waiting for them at Lake Moan?

ISBN: 978-1-62285-003-7

ZOMBIE FIELD DAY
ZOMBIE ZAPPERS BOOK 2

Join the Zombie Zappers back at school for the next round of zombie mayhem. When Rotfield Middle School students start turning into zombies, Leo and his friends are the only ones who might be able to save them. Can they discover the cause of this outbreak before it's too late?

ISBN: 978-1-62285-005-1

THE ZOMBIE NEXT DOOR
ZOMBIE ZAPPERS BOOK 3

What if your next-door neighbor were a zombie? The Zombie Zappers return to find out exactly why Leo's neighbor is acting so strange in this suspenseful book. Leo learns a valuable lesson in the process.

ISBN: 978-1-62285-010-5

DOWN, ZOMBIE, DOWN!
ZOMBIE ZAPPERS BOOK 4

The Zombie Zappers jump back into action when a unique zombie outbreak spreads to their hometown. Leo will have to join forces with Chad's new best friend if they want to stop Rotfield from being overrun by a new breed of zombie.

ISBN: 978-1-62285-015-0